SeedPower

Discovering How Plants Grow

by Anna Prokos • illustrated by Dave Clegg

Imagine That! books are produced and published by Red Chair Press

Red Chair Press LLC   PO Box 333   South Egremont, MA 01258-0333

www.redchairpress.com

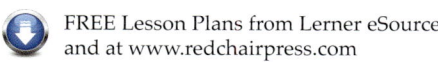 FREE Lesson Plans from Lerner eSource
and at www.redchairpress.com

Publisher's Cataloging-In-Publication Data
(Prepared by The Donohue Group, Inc.)

Names: Prokos, Anna. | Clegg, Dave, illustrator.
Title: Seed power : discovering how plants grow / by Anna Prokos ; illustrated by Dave Clegg.

Description: South Egremont, MA : Red Chair Press, [2017] | Imagine that! | Interest age level: 006-009. | Includes Fact File data, a glossary and references for additional reading. | Includes bibliographical references and index. | Summary: "Have you ever swallowed a seed? If you've eaten a strawberry or a tomato, the answer is, yes! But why didn't a new plant grow inside your stomach? In this book, readers discover what a seed needs to grow into a fruit-bearing plant."-- Provided by publisher.

Identifiers: LCCN 2016934111 | ISBN 978-1-63440-151-7 (library hardcover) | ISBN 978-1-63440-157-9 (paperback) | ISBN 978-1-63440-163-0 (ebook)

Subjects: LCSH: Seeds--Growth--Juvenile literature. | Growth (Plants)--Juvenile literature. CYAC: Seeds. | Growth (Plants)

Classification: LCC QK711.5 .P76 2017 (print) | LCC QK711.5 (ebook) | DDC 580--dc23

Copyright © 2017 Red Chair Press LLC
RED CHAIR PRESS, the RED CHAIR and associated logos are registered trademarks of Red Chair Press LLC.

All rights reserved. No part of this book may be reproduced, stored in an information or retrieval system, or transmitted in any form by any means, electronic, mechanical including photocopying, recording, or otherwise without the prior written permission from the Publisher. For permissions, contact info@redchairpress.com

Technical charts by Joe LeMonnier

Photo credits: Shutterstock, Inc

First Edition by:
Red Chair Press LLC   PO Box 333   South Egremont, MA 01258-0333

Printed in the United States of America
Distributed in the U.S. by Lerner Publisher Services. www.lernerbooks.com

1116 1P CGBS17

Between cracks in a sidewalk and even out of rain gutters, it seems like plants can grow just about anywhere. Some plants grow by sending runners from their roots. But that may be how the plant gets larger or spreads to a bigger area (think about how grass grows). But even grass plants started with a seed.

Are you ready to discover what else a plant needs to grow into strong healthy plants?

Table of Contents

Exploration Begins. 4

Fact File 26

Words to Keep 31

Learn More at the Library 32

Index 32

Connor licked his lips. He couldn't wait to bite into the juicy slice of watermelon. It was his favorite fruit, especially in the summer.

"Who's ready to play?" the host asked. The crowd cheered. Connor was ready to win the watermelon-eating race.

"There's only one rule," the announcer explained. "You must spit the seeds—but not at me!" The racers laughed.

IT'S A FACT
Watermelons are 92% water.

The contestants checked their melon wedges. Connor didn't notice any seeds. "Go!" the announcer blasted. The kids started slurping swiftly.

7

Connor took a giant bite of the juicy slice. His taste buds burst with happiness. Yum! He chewed the chunk quickly and took another bite.

Seed! The slippery seed swirled in his mouth. Connor tried to spit it out. But the sneaky speck slipped down his throat. Oh no! "Will a watermelon grow in my belly?" Connor wondered.

Suddenly, the crowd disappeared. So did his watermelon slice! Connor wasn't at the contest. He was at a farm!

IT'S A FACT

The U.S. ranks 5th in the production of watermelons worldwide. Watermelons are grown in 44 states.

A man in overalls shook his hand.
"Welcome to Sowing Seeds Farm," he said.
"We **sow** seeds and watch them bloom."

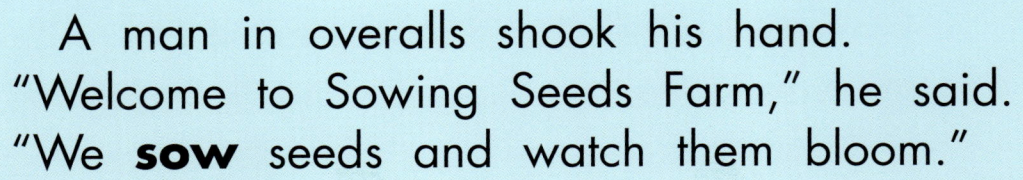

"How do you sow a seed?" Connor asked.
"Is it like sewing a button?"

"Not quite!" the farmer explained. "When you sew a button, you attach it with thread. When you sow a seed, you plant it in the ground."

Connor remembered the seed he swallowed. "Can a seed sow in my stomach?" he asked.

IT'S A FACT

Some farmers grow a variety of seedless melons.

"That's a funny question," the farmer laughed. "Seeds need water and a good spot to grow. Your belly is not a good place for a seed to germinate. But soil is—come take a look."